walking home

DOUBLEDAY CANADA BOOKS BY ERIC WALTERS

We All Fall Down
United We Stand
Safe As Houses
Wave
Alexandria of Africa
Tell Me Why
Beverly Hills Maasai
Shaken
End of Days
The Taming (with Teresa Toten)

walking home

ERIC WALTERS

DOUBLEDAY
CANADA

Doubleday Canada and colophon are registered trademarks
of Random House of Canada Limited

Library and Archives Canada Cataloguing in Publication

Walters, Eric, 1957-, author
Walking home / Eric Walters.

Issued in print and electronic formats.
ISBN 978-0-385-68157-5 (pbk.) ISBN 978-0-385-68158-2 (epub)

I. Title.

PS8595.A598W34 2014   jC813'.54   C2014-903133-5
                                                C2014-903134-3

Issued in print and electronic formats.

This book is a work of fiction. Names, characters, places and incidents are
products of the author's imagination or are used fictitiously. Any resemblance to
actual events or locales or persons, living or dead, is entirely coincidental.

Cover image: © Ajn / Dreamstime.com
Cover design: Jennifer Lum
Printed and bound in the USA

Published in Canada by Doubleday Canada,
a division of Random House of Canada Limited,
a Penguin Random House Company
www.randomhouse.ca

10 9 8 7 6 5 4